This
Harry
book belongs to

....

SCELIDOSAURUS

(ske-LI-doh-SAW-rus)

TYRANNOSAURUS

(tie-RAN-oh-SAW-rus)

TRICERATOPS

(try-SER-a-tops)

STEGOSAURUS

(STEG-oh-SAW-rus)

PTERODACTYL

(TER-oh-DAC-til)

APATOSAURUS

(a-PAT-oh-SAW-rus)

ANCHISAURUS

(AN-ki-SAW-rus)

For Edward Matthew Traynor
I.W.

For Aonghas and Mairead
A.R.

PUFFIN BOOKS
Published by the Penguin Group
Penguin Books Ltd, 80 Strand, London WC2R 0RL, England
Penguin Group (USA) Inc., 375 Hudson Street, New York, New York 10014, USA
Penguin Group (Canada), 10 Alcorn Avenue, Toronto, Ontario, Canada M4V 3B2 (a division of Pearson Penguin Canada Inc.)
Penguin Ireland, 25 St Stephen's Green, Dublin 2, Ireland (a division of Penguin Books Ltd)
Penguin Group (Australia), 250 Camberwell Road, Camberwell, Victoria 3124, Australia (a division of Pearson Australia Group Pty Ltd)
Penguin Books India Pvt Ltd, 11 Community Centre, Panchsheel Park, New Delhi – 110 017, India
Penguin Group (NZ), cnr Airborne and Rosedale Roads, Albany, Auckland 1310, New Zealand (a division of Pearson New Zealand Ltd)
Penguin Books (South Africa) (Pty) Ltd, 24 Sturdee Avenue, Rosebank, Johannesburg 2196, South Africa

Penguin Books Ltd, Registered Offices: 80 Strand, London WC2R 0RL, England

www.penguin.com

First published 2004
Published in this edition 2005
7 9 10 8

British Library Cataloguing in Publication Data
A CIP catalogue record for this book is available from the British Library

ISBN–13: 978–0–14056–953–7
ISBN–10: 0–14056–953–7

Harry and the Dinosaurs at the Museum

Ian Whybrow and Adrian Reynolds

PUFFIN

Sam wanted Mum to take her to the museum.
She had to study the Romans for homework.
"What are Romans?" asked Harry.

Sam said they were our ancestors, but he was
too young to understand.
  Harry wanted to take the dinosaurs to see them.

Sam said, "No way!"
She said Harry would just get bored and silly.
That was why Sam's homework got smudged.

Mum made them both settle down.
She said a museum would be a fine
outing for everybody.
"I'd love to go," said Nan.

The museum was bigger than a hospital.
You had to have a map.

On the way to the Romans, they passed the cavemen.

"Are these ancestors?" asked Harry.

Mum said yes, everybody in the world came from cavemen.
They lit fires and did hunting.

Harry liked the stone axes!

The dinosaurs liked the
sabre-toothed tiger!
Raaah! Sharp teeth!

Next stop was the Egyptians.
  They saw mummies in boxes and funny
writing like pictures.
  "Are Egyptians ancestors?" asked Harry.
  "Yes, but not the right ones," said Sam. "We
want the Romans. Come on, hurry up!"

Finally they reached the Romans.
They had good swords and spears,
and helmets with brushes on.

But what a lot of old pots, broken ones too!
  Sam started doing drawing.
  "We've seen the Romans now," said Harry.
"I'm hungry! Let's go!"

"Raaah! Anchisaurus pinched me!" said Stegosaurus.
"He's taking up all the room!" said Anchisaurus.
"Behave!" said Harry in a loud voice.
"Look, Harry *is* being silly!" groaned Sam. "I knew it!"

"I think the dinosaurs need a run about," said Harry.
Mum said better not. They might get lost.
"Come on, let's get something to eat," she said.
"Afterwards we'll come back here, so Sam
can finish her studies."

The cafeteria was very busy. Nan and Harry
and the dinosaurs waited at a table while
Mum and Sam went to queue up.

"Look, I'm a caveman! Raaah!" said Triceratops.
"Look, I'm a Roman! Raaah!" said Pterodactyl.
"Look, I'm a mummy! Raaah!" said Tyrannosaurus.

After lunch, everyone felt a lot better and they
set off back to the Romans.
   But it wasn't long before Anchisaurus got bored.
"I'm bored too!" said Tyrannosaurus.

"Never mind," said Harry, "it's your turn to do studying. Pay attention, my dinosaurs."
He taught them Climbing Up Display Cases.
Then taught them Sliding On The Slippery Floor.

That was how they got lost.

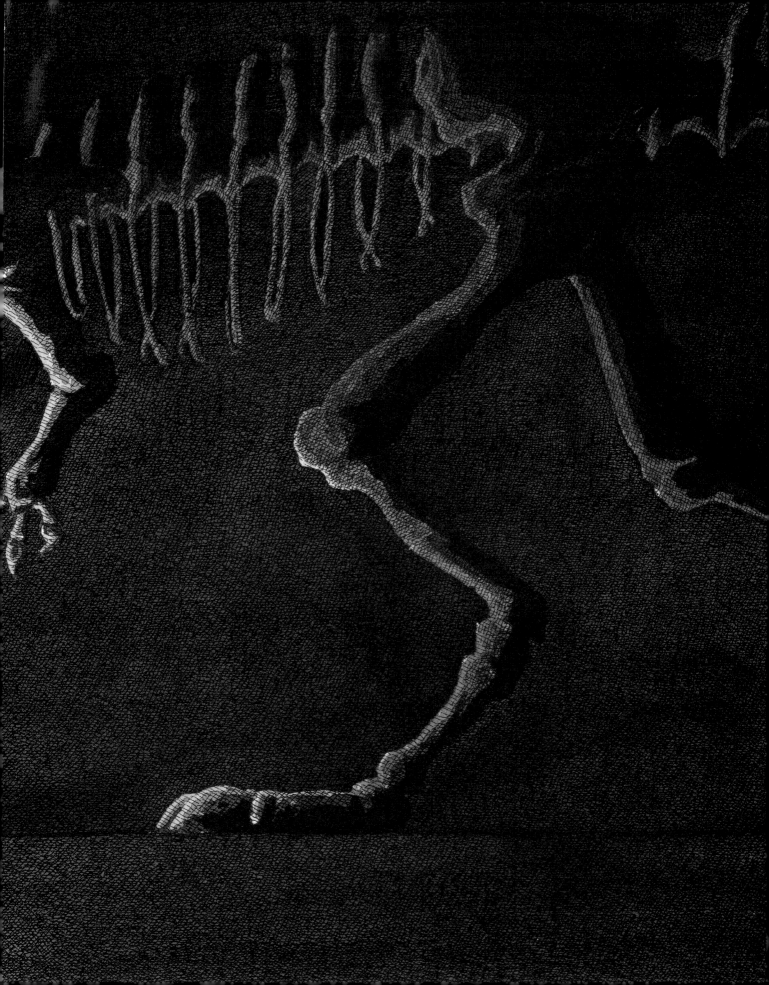

"Oh no! Where's Harry?" said Mum. "Quick! Let's find the person in charge!"

Sam said Harry was stupid. "I bet he's gone off on a bus!" she said.

"Nonsense!" said Nan. "I know where we'll find him!"

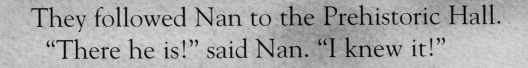

They followed Nan to the Prehistoric Hall. "There he is!" said Nan. "I knew it!"

Harry was still teaching his dinosaurs.
"Boys come from cavemen and Romans and Egyptians,"
he explained. "But these are *your* ancestors."

So Tyrannosaurus said "Raaah!" to his ancestor.
  So did Apatosaurus and Scelidosaurus and Triceratops
and the rest of the bucketful of dinosaurs.
  All except Pterodactyl, who gave his ancestor a nose-rub.

"Now, young man!" said the person in charge.
"We had better look for your mum. Could you
tell me your name?"

Harry said his name, address and telephone
number, no problem at all.
  All the people said very good, clever boy!
  Nan rushed over. "He's with us!" she called proudly.

"Harry!" said Mum. "We thought we'd lost you!"

"I wasn't lost!" said Harry. "I was with my dinosaurs."

"And we were with our ancestors," said the dinosaurs. RAAAAH!

ENDOSAURUS

SCELIDOSAURUS

(ske-LI-doh-SAW-rus)

TYRANNOSAURUS

(tie-RAN-oh-SAW-rus)

TRICERATOPS

(try-SER-a-tops)

STEGOSAURUS

(STEG-oh-SAW-rus)

PTERODACTYL

(TER-oh-DAC-til)

APATOSAURUS

(a-PAT-oh-SAW-rus)

ANCHISAURUS

(AN-ki-SAW-rus)

SCELIDOSAURUS

(ske-LI-doh-SAW-rus)

TYRANNOSAURUS

(tie-RAN-oh-SAW-rus)

TRICERATOPS

(try-SER-a-tops)

STEGOSAURUS

(STEG-oh-SAW-rus)

PTERODACTYL

(TER-oh-DAC-til)

APATOSAURUS

(a-PAT-oh-SAW-rus)

ANCHISAURUS

(AN-ki-SAW-rus)

Look out for all of Harry's adventures!

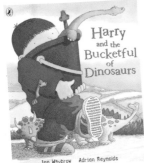

Harry and the Bucketful of Dinosaurs
Harry finds some old plastic dinosaurs and cleans them, finds out their names and takes them everywhere with him – until, one day, they get lost…Will he ever find them?

ISBN 0140569804

Harry and the Snow King
There's just enough snow for Harry to build a very small snow king. But then the snow king disappears – who's kidnapped him?

ISBN 0140569863

Harry and the Robots
Harry's robot is sent to the toy hospital to be fixed, so Harry and Nan decide to make a new one. When Nan has to go to hospital, Harry knows just how to help her get better!

ISBN 0140569820

Harry and the Dinosaurs say "Raahh!"
Harry's dinosaurs are acting strangely. They're hiding all over the house, refusing to come out…Could it be because today is the day of Harry's dentist appointment?

ISBN 0140569812

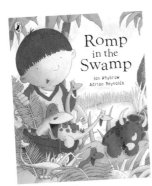

Romp in the Swamp
Harry has to play at Charlie's house and doesn't want to share his dinosaurs. But when Charlie builds a fantastic swamp, Harry and the dinosaurs can't help but join in the fun!

ISBN 0140569847

Harry and the Dinosaurs make a Christmas Wish
Harry and the dinosaurs would *love* to own a duckling. They wait till Christmas and make a special wish, but Santa leaves them something even more exciting…!

ISBN 0141380179 (hbk)
ISBN 0140569529 (pbk)

ISBN 0140569839

ISBN 0140569855

Harry and the Dinosaurs play Hide-and-Seek
Harry and the Dinosaurs have a Very Busy Day
Join in with Harry and his dinosaurs for some peep-through fold-out fun! These exciting books about shapes and colours make learning easy!